"Revenge is a dish drink ~~dish~~ best served cold."

Baa Baa was here

For Jas, Mizz & Brendan

MIX
Paper from
responsible sources
FSC™ C020056

First U.S. edition 2016. Library of Congress Catalog Card Number pending. ISBN 978-0-7636-8067-1.
This book was hand-lettered. The illustrations were done in pencil and rendered digitally.
Candlewick Press, 99 Dover Street, Somerville, Massachusetts 02144. visit us at www.candlewick.com.
Printed in Heshan, Guangdong, China. 16 17 18 19 21 LEO 10 9 8 7 6 5 4 3 2 1

CANDLEWICK PRESS

I LOVE LEMONADE

Mark Sommerset
illustrated by Rowan Sommerset

Quirky Turkey wanted revenge.

Sweet revenge.

When along came Little Baa Baa.

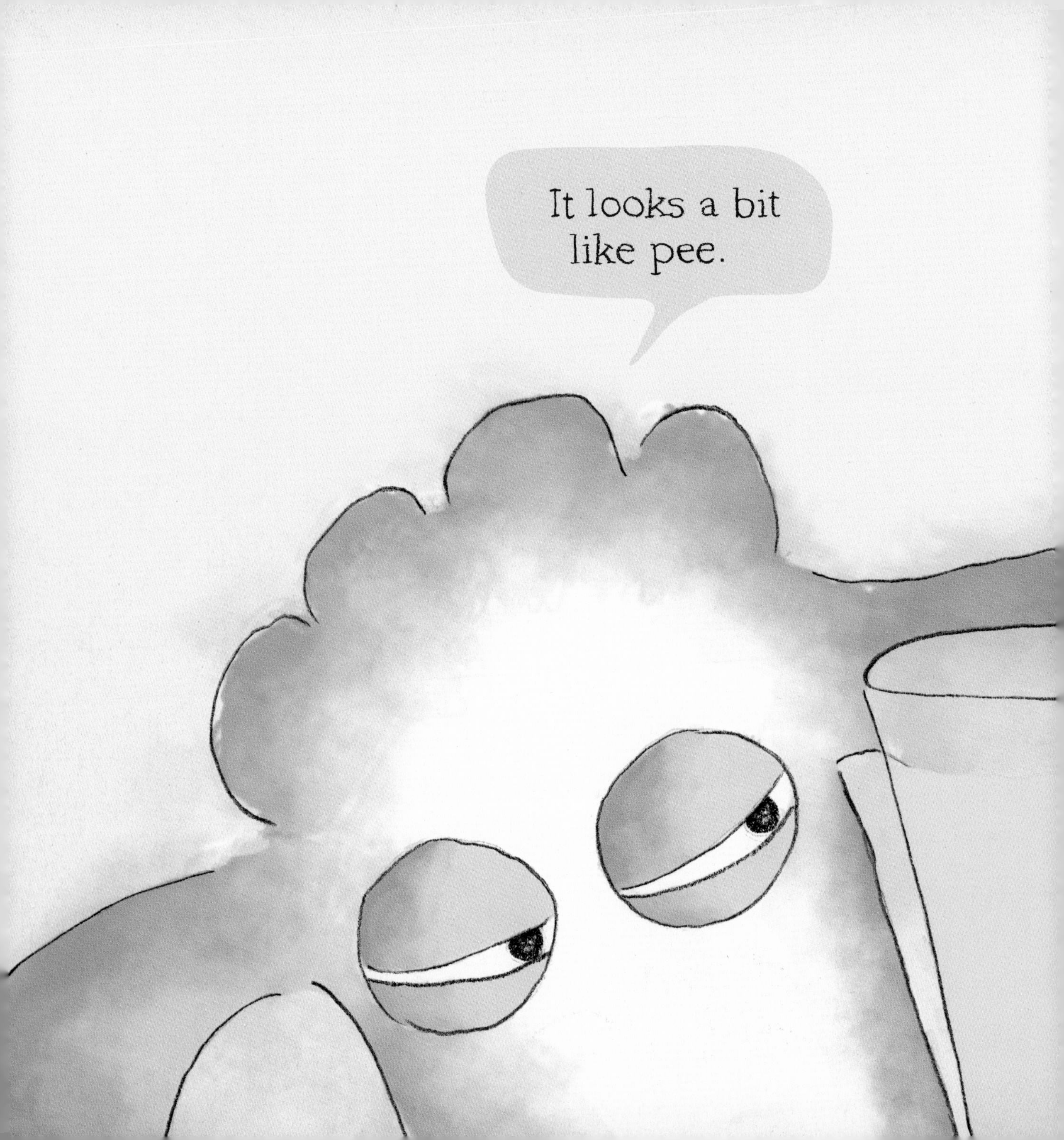
It looks a bit like pee.

So, you're sure it's lemonade?

Yes, it's lemonade.

That's fresh.

And squeezed.

And delicious.

And free!

To sheep.

And turkeys!

YOU'RE a turkey!

guzzle!

guzzle!

guzzle!